Connect with Your Heavenly Father

DOUGLAS PYSZKA

Published, April 2019
Fiona Inc.
Hummelstown, PA
www.fionainc.com
717-917-8101

Unless otherwise identified, Bible quotations in this book are from the Amplified, New Living Translation (NLT) and the King James versions of the Bible.

CONTENTS

ACKNOWLEDGMENTS

I want to thank my heavenly Father, God, who I am gratefully connected to. He gave me His Son, Jesus, Whom I have made my Savior, Lord, Master and King. My Father also empowered me by His Holy Spirit to do all that He called me to do.

I also appreciate my wonderful wife, Fiona, who is my soul mate, best friend and co-laborer in the work of God's kingdom. She inspires me in so many ways. I am thankful to be a father of two wonderful boys, Gabriel and Josiah. They are a source of joy in my life and I am blessed to watch them become all that God wants them to be.

Thanks goes to my father, Arthur Pyszka, as I was privileged to grow up in a loving home with a good and loving father and mother, Barb, whom I love. God has been good to me.

A special thanks goes to Lisa Schmidt who helped me to say the right thing in the right way. She makes sure my "I's" are dotted and my "t's" crossed.

INTRODUCTION

Ways To Connect To Your Heavenly Father

For the past thirty-seven years, I have experienced a connection to God as my Father. There were times in my life when I had a strong connection and there were times in my life when my connection to Him was not what it could be. I have been serving in a position that God has placed me in doing His work, proclaiming His good news and helping people find their inheritance and treasure in God's Word. I would like you to consider your relationship with God. Is it where you would like it to be or would you like to draw even closer to God? Either way, let's take this journey to connect to the heavenly Father.

Everyone needs a strong connection with God because He is the source of life and good things. Our connection to God as Father is made stronger by continuing to be in a loving and devoted relationship with Him.

The devotions you will read have been taken from the gospel of John and they reveal ways that Jesus was connected to His Father. Knowing how Jesus connected to His heavenly Father will help strengthen your connection to Him.

In the beginning, man had a strong connection to God, but that connection was severed by sin. Sin separated God and man, disrupted their fellowship and disconnected the relationship they had. Mankind needed help to reestablish a close connection with God. Jesus was sent to earth by God as a man, to repair the breech and to bridge the gap that separated us from the heavenly Father. Jesus reestablished God and man's connection through His life, death, burial and resurrection.

Jesus is the Master key, the only door and the gatekeeper that leads directly to the heavenly Father. Jesus is the entrance to the Almighty. Jesus had a strong connection with His Father, and He is the only link by which anyone can connect to God. He came to show us the only way to the Father by seeking and saving the lost; doing His Father's will; showing us who His Father is and helping us establish a close relationship with His Father.

Connecting with God begins with a desire to know Him. You have an adversary, the devil, who opposes and interferes with your relationship with God and tries to prevent you from knowing your heavenly Father by stealing, killing and destroying you. Your relationship with God gives you victory over the devil and stops his wicked plan from occurring.

God loves you and wants to have a close intimate relationship with you. When you're connected to God, you have eternal life, you understand your purpose and you are fulfilled and content. You find out who you are, why you exist and where you are going. Everyone should be connected to God and to know Him as Father. Enjoy connecting with your heavenly Father.

1
CONNECT BY RECEIVING THE LOVE HE HAS FOR YOU

John 3:35 **The Father loves the Son** and has given all things into His hands

Think about those powerful words, "The Father loves the Son." These words are very potent. God loves you the same way that He loves Jesus. The Son represents you, the Father loves the Son, so the Father loves you. I know it's hard to believe that God loves you the same way as He does Jesus, but He really does.

Receiving God's love for you comes simply by choosing to receive it. Believe in the love that God has for you. Jesus connected to His Father through mutual love they shared for each other and you can also have that mutual love like Jesus has. It is possible to be rooted, grounded and cemented in God's love. There is nothing that will stop God from loving you! Simply choose to love Him back.

God showed the world how much He loved by giving them His only Son, and the world could connect to Him through Jesus. Know and believe the love that God has for you. God is love; whoever abides in love abides in God, and God in him. God loves you and shows His affection for you in practical ways. He talks with you, helps you, strengthens you and leads you through life. God's love for you is powerful and undeniable, demonstrated in Christ.

You can also see in this verse that love gives freely and lavishly. The Father loved the Son and gave all things into His hands. God loves you because He gives you things like a Savior, grace, forgiveness and love. When you love someone, you give to them.

Tell God that you love Him, and show Him by believing Him, following Him and serving Him. Let God be the object of your unconditional love, which decides the direction and character of your life.

Prayer: Father, thank you for being love and showing love to me. You loved me and gave me Jesus. I receive Jesus, Your gift of love. Father, I love You. Increase my understanding, insight, and operation in your love. I yield to Your Holy Spirit and allow Your love to flow through me in greater ways. Thank You for showing me how to truly love. I trust and rest in Your love in Jesus' Name.

2

CONNECT THROUGH SPIRIT-LED AND TRUTH-GROUNDED WORSHIP

John 4:21-24 Jesus told her, "Believe Me, woman, an hour is coming when you will worship the Father neither on this mountain nor in Jerusalem. 22 You Samaritans worship what you do not know. We worship what we do know, because salvation is from the Jews. 23 But an hour is coming, & is now here, when **the true worshipers will worship the Father in spirit & truth**. Yes, **the Father wants such people to worship Him**. 24 God is spirit, & those who worship Him must worship in spirit & truth."

Have you ever had a relationship that did not work out? It is painful, hurtful and confusing. Maybe you even had several failed relationships. A track record of broken relationships can skew your image of what a good relationship looks like and you may feel that you are destined to be lonely. Experiences like these can cause you to think you would not even qualify to have a relationship with God. If you have felt like that, there is hope for you.

Jesus spoke to a woman who was disconnected from God, looking for true love but not finding it. She failed to succeed in many relationships, even being married and divorced five times. I imagine her heart was broken, and she tried to fill that void in her heart with the wrong things. She may have even lost hope. Jesus met her at a well to tell her about a living water and to introduce her to His Father.

Jesus touched this woman's heart. He offered her a gift of God, something that would truly satisfy her thirst and give her what she longed for, a fountain of water springing up to eternal life. He gave her hope. He told her the kind of worshiper she could be, and the kind of worshiper the Father is looking for. This woman believed what Jesus said and told others about Him. Jesus told her that His Father loved her and wanted to connect with her through worship, just like He wants to connect to you through worship.

Worship is expressing your heartfelt love and enthusiasm to God for who He is and what He has done. To worship God is to honor Him, give Him reverence and respect and yield to Him. God gave His Word to you as a guide to show you how to worship Him. Believe what He says and love Him, worship Him and you will be connected to Him.

Prayer: Heavenly Father, in Jesus' name I come to you and drink of your living water. I believe Your message and worship You with all my heart, soul and strength. I acknowledge You in all things and I place my trust in You. Lead me in the way that I should go and help me to please you. I bless Your holy name!

3
CONNECT BY IDENTIFYING WITH HIM

John 5:16-18 Therefore, the Jews began persecuting Jesus because He was doing these things on the Sabbath. 17 But Jesus responded to them, "My Fathers is still working, and I am working also." 18 This is why the Jews began trying even more to kill Him: Not only was He breaking the Sabbath, but **He was even calling God His own Father, making Himself equal with God**.

Have you ever wondered where you came from and why you exist? Every design has a designer. Every product finds its purpose from its maker. God is the one who designed, created and formed you. He has made you on purpose for a divine purpose. As you identify with your heavenly Father, you'll realize your purpose so you can fulfill it.

Imagine how difficult it is when a person loses their identity or memory and does not know who they are or where they came from. It is like a person struck with amnesia. Although it may be temporary, they forget many important things about themselves and they do not recognize family or friends. I imagine that would be confusing and frustrating. They desperately try to figure out who they are and what they are supposed to do. Not knowing God as Father can be just as confusing and frustrating. Once you know God you will realize your true identity, and you will remember the important things He says about you.

As you connect to your heavenly Father by accepting Jesus as your Savior, you proclaim God is your Father and you identify yourself as a child of God in His family with His DNA in you. Jesus identified Himself as God's Son, called God His Father, and proclaimed to share His nature and characteristics.

You discover more about what God thinks about you by believing that what He said about you in His Word is true. You recognize that God created you, loves you, called you according to His purpose and united you with Him. A connection with God improves your life.

Prayer: Father, I am committed to knowing you and doing what You have called me to do. I thank You for creating me and giving me a divine purpose. I believe Your report because Your Words are true. Without You and apart from You I can do nothing. Lead, guide and direct me on the right path. I Love Your Word it is my source of life in Jesus' name.

4
CONNECT BY ACCOMPLISHING HIS WORK

John 5:36 "I have a greater testimony than John's because of **the works that the Father has given Me to accomplish**. These very works I am doing testify about Me that the Father has sent Me.
John 10:37-38 Jesus said, "Believe the works. **By doing God's works you will know and understand the Father** is in Me and I in the Father."

God calls everyone to serve Him in various ways and in various positions. Jesus recognized His Father's work and how He worked through Him. God the Father worked through Jesus as Jesus made the blind see, the lame walk, lepers cleansed, the deaf to hear, the poor to receive the gospel and the world saved. Doing what the Lord tells you to do, going where He tells you to go and being who He tells you to be reveals the strength of your connection to Him.

God knows why He designed you. God gave you talents, skills and abilities for His own purpose and He assigns you to the position He made you for. Having a vibrant, intimate relationship with God is a key to discovering your God-given purpose. Talk with God and listen to Him and you'll discover the reason you exist.

God's purpose for me is to help people find their inheritance and treasure in God's Word through teaching and preaching the gospel of Jesus Christ. I get excited when I see people receive God's Word, apply it and practice it in their life.

Everyone's assignment is unique. The Bible is full of people just like you who discovered their purpose and accomplished it. God told Adam to take care of the garden and keep it. God assigned Noah to build a very large boat to save humanity. The Lord called Abraham and Sarah to birth nations. The heavenly Father assigned Esther to be a queen of a foreign nation to save the Jews. God called Daniel to be a prophetic statesman in Babylon. God reveals His heavenly purpose to everyone who is connected to Him.

Prayer: Heavenly Father, I come to you in Jesus' name. Thank you for calling me with a holy calling and giving me the strength and grace to walk worthy of my calling. Help me to discover my heavenly purpose. I will do the work that You give me to do. I am here to please you more than anyone else. I will use my gifts, talents and abilities for you and what you have assigned me to do. I repent for any area that I have disobeyed you and ask you to forgive me. Today, I will do what you say with all my heart.

5
CONNECT BY KEEPING YOUR EYES FOCUSED ON HIM

John 5:19-20 Then Jesus replied, "I assure you: **The Son is not able to do anything on His own, but only what He sees the Father doing**. For whatever the Father does, the Son also does these things in the same way. 20 For **the Father loves the Son & shows Him everything He is doing**, & He will show Him greater works than these so that you will be amazed.

Keep your focus on is Jesus and the eternal life that He gives to all who believe in Him. Fix your eyes on Jesus your whole life. As you focus on Him, you will have God's presence that will help you do great things.

God wants you to imitate Him just like Jesus imitated His Father. Imitating a person requires focus. Remember the games, "Follow the Leader and Simon Says"? Each game had a leader and required you to focus on the leader. You had to watch what they did and listen to what they said so you could imitate them. Jesus followed the leader, His Father. Jesus saw His Father heal people and Jesus healed people. Jesus saw His Father feed people and Jesus fed multitudes. Jesus also saw and heard His Father teach and Jesus taught people what His Father taught. The Father loved the Son and showed Him everything He did.

When you focus on God you are looking at Perfect Love. Perfect Love shows you everything you need to know. It says what is on its heart and shares its secrets with you. The Father loves the Son and shows Him all things and the Father loves you and wants to show you what is in His heart too. As you look to God, He will show you everything so you can do what you see and connect with Him.

You can do amazing things simply by looking and listening to God and doing what you see Him do and hear Him say. The more you look to God, the greater things you will be able to do.

Prayer: Father, open my eyes that I may see you. Give me clear vision. I look to you because You are the Author and Finisher of my faith. As I look to You and Your Word, I can practice it in my life. I desire to pattern my life after you. Thank you for revealing Yourself to me. I love you Lord, in Jesus' name.

6
CONNECT BY SEEKING HIS WILL

John 5:30 "I can do nothing on My own. I judge only as I hear, and My judgment is righteous, because **I do not seek My own will, but the will of Him who sent Me**.

Imagine a person who does not seek his or her own will. What qualities would be necessary not to seek your own will? You would have to be selfless, be able to put another before yourself, without pride and content to be able to serve. That is what Jesus did with His Father. Jesus focused His mind, will, emotions and strength completely on doing what His Father sent Him to do. That is a great way to connect to your heavenly Father. Those who you are committed to, you are connected to.

What was God's will for Jesus? God desired for Jesus to come to earth to seek and save the lost, and to give His life a ransom for many. Jesus completely relied on His Father to complete His assignment. Even though He was pressured, tempted and persecuted to do His own will, He only did God's will. Everyone can choose to do God's will.

God gave you a free will and you are free to choose what is right or what is wrong. God does not interfere with your will, your ability to choose, and He does not force you to do what He wants. He loves you, and He wants you to love Him freely. Jesus chose to seek His Father's will and had a strong bond with His Father.

God's Word is His will and it is where He reveals Himself, His plans, His kingdom and what He likes and doesn't like. God's Word is His gift to you and when you choose to seek it and follow it you will be blessed, safe and protected.

Making a strong commitment to God opens the door for you to God's heart where He shares His goals and desires with you. Jesus sought His Father's will and accomplished His Father's will. He and His Father did everything together and made a way for you to follow His example.

Prayer: Father, I recognize that You have a will and a purpose for my life. I receive Your design for me. I will follow You and obey Your word. I set my heart on seeking You and Your will. You are everything I need, want and desire. Thank you, Lord for revealing to me my assignment on earth. You created me and called me, and I will answer Your call and serve You with all my heart. Thank you for making my path clear and leading me by Your light. In the name of Jesus.

7

CONNECT BY ACCEPTING JESUS AS YOUR LORD

John 5:39-44 You pore over the Scriptures because you presume that by them you possess eternal life. **These are the very words that testify about Me**, 40 yet you refuse to come to Me to have life. 41 I do not accept glory from men, 42 but I know you, that you do not have the love of God within you. 43 I have come in My Father's name, and you have not received Me; but if someone else comes in his own name, you will receive him. 44 How can you believe if you accept glory from one another, yet do not seek the glory that comes from the only God?

Jesus addressed a group of people who did not believe in Him, refused to come to Him and did not receive Him. The only way to get to the Father is to come to Jesus, believe in Him and receive Him into your heart. People without Jesus are without God and do not really understand what kind of shape they are in, it's a path that leads to destruction.

Accepting Jesus as Lord ushers you into God's kingdom, family and house. My last name is Pyszka because I was born into the Pyszka family. I have the privilege of carrying on the Pyszka name. Jesus came in His Father's name and by accepting Jesus as your Lord, you can access all the benefits that are available in that name.

Being connected with Father God has so many benefits including eternal life, a way to prosper and increase through His blessing, a solid rock to stand on that stays put even in storms, a love that never fails, forgiveness that removes guilt, shame and condemnation and an eternal inheritance and so many more.

God made accepting Jesus easy, it is done through love. God sends His good news into the earth, you hear it, believe it, accept and it instantly becomes yours. A relationship with God is like a marriage relationship. I love my wife but there was a time when she was not my wife. After getting to know her, I fell in love with her and I desired to know her exclusively and intimately. I asked her to marry me and she said yes! We continue to remain committed to each other and take steps to guard our relationship. That is what we must do with our heavenly Father. Once we meet Him, we must continue to remain close to Him, and follow Him till we finish our course and complete the race.

Prayer: Heavenly Father, I love Jesus, I love You and I love your Spirit. I give You my heart. I invite You into my life and I surrender control and allow You to have Your way in me. Reveal Yourself to me. I trust You with all my heart and I lean not to my own understanding. I believe in You. Thank You for giving Jesus to me. He is my Savior.

8
CONNECT BY COMING TO HIM AND RECEIVING THE REAL BREAD

John 6:32-35 Jesus said to them, "I assure you: Moses didn't give you the bread from heaven, but **My Father gives you the real bread from heaven**. 33 For the bread of God is the One who comes down from heaven and gives life to the world." V. 35-40 **"I am the bread of life," Jesus told them**. "No one who comes to Me will ever be hungry, & no one who believes in Me will ever be thirsty again.

What do you do when you are hungry and have access to food? You come to where the food is, you sit down, and you eat until you are fully satisfied. Jesus is like heavenly bread. You can come to Him, take Him into your heart like you would take in a freshly baked slice of homemade bread. God's heavenly bread certainly has greater benefits than the bread that man makes.

Bread is often described as a basic source of life. People can survive on bread and water. I love homemade bread. I love its aroma, its texture and how it melts butter when it is hot. It is made of simple ingredients such as flour, yeast, water, sugar, salt and oil, and supplies energy to your physical body. There is a more satisfying bread that comes from heaven and its main ingredient is divine love. This bread gives life to the world, a necessary ingredient to remain connected to your heavenly Father.

Jesus called Himself the "Bread of Life." Just as physical Bread gets in you and becomes a part of you when you eat it, Jesus becomes a part of you when you receive Him in your heart and life. He will sustain and satisfy you with His kindness, faithfulness, compassion, love and power. When you take in the heavenly bread, you partake in God's divine nature. His character and life are disbursed in your heart and you can live with Him forever, doing His will all your days. Partake of the bread of heaven today. Come get some!

Prayer: Father, I thank you for giving to me the Bread of Life, your Son Jesus. I will feast on your goodness forever. Thank You for sustaining, satisfying and strengthening me. Jesus, You are my life. I dedicate my whole being to follow You and carry out Your plan. I am Yours and You are mine!

9
CONNECT BY LEARNING FROM HIM
AND LISTENING TO HIM

John 6:43-46 Jesus answered them, "Stop complaining among yourselves. 44 No one can come to Me unless the Father who sent Me draws him, & I will raise him up on the last day. 45 It is written in the Prophets: They will all be taught by God. **Everyone who has listened to & learned from the Father comes to Me** - 46 not that anyone has seen the Father except the One who is from God. He has seen the Father.

God the Father knows all things and wants to share His knowledge with you. We can learn from Him simply by listening to what He says. God draws you to Himself because He loves you and wants a relationship with you. Jesus is a master communicator, the greatest teacher ever. He speaks every language and can reach the highly educated and the uneducated. Jesus wants to teach you about His Father and how His kingdom operates. Open your heart and learn from Him by listening to Him.

Multitudes of people were attracted to Jesus when He walked the earth, and many continue to come to Him today. The more I learn about God, the more I want to know. God's Holy Spirit is Jesus' promoter drawing people to the Savior through God's love and grace.

Jesus gives private and public lessons to those who want to learn. His public lessons are conducted in church. His private lessons are carried out in personal prayer, worship and praise. The Lord invites all those who love Him into His holy presence. It is in those intimate times that He teaches you truths and shows you things to come. Jesus is a gentle and patient teacher who shares greater truths to those who seek Him wholeheartedly.

You can truly know the Lord by following Him as He draws you in. Go after God, you will not be disappointed. Learning about God comes from an intimate relationship with Him and the closer you get to Him the easier it is to hear His voice and do what He says. As you listen to God's voice and learn His ways, you will be closely connected to Him.

Prayer: Heavenly Father, I am a teachable person who is willing to listen to You and learn from You. Be my Mentor, Teacher and Guide. You lead me on the path of righteousness, a well-lit path, for Your name's sake. I come to You and I listen to Your words. Your words are true, and they give me life. Give me ears to hear what Your Spirit is saying to me. Help me to understand the ways of Your kingdom. Jesus, show me the Father, in the name of Jesus.

10
CONNECT BY FEEDING ON HIS WORD AND LIVING FOR HIM

John 6:57 57 Just as the living Father sent Me & I live because of the Father, so **the one who feeds on Me will live because of Me.**

Jesus encouraged people to feed on Him by eating His flesh and drinking His blood to receive eternal life. He was not referring to cannibalism in anyway. His flesh is His Word and His blood is His redeeming love and forgiveness He bestowed on all.

What you eat goes into you and becomes a part of you. You take a bite of food, chew it, swallow it and it is digested into your body. An unbalanced diet is eating only junk food, food that has no nutritional value, and it will negatively affect your physical body eventually leading to poor health. A balanced diet is eating a variety of fruits, vegetables, grains, proteins and good fat and not over-indulging in anything, but eating sensibly. A balanced diet will enhance your health.

Feeding on God's Word consists of reading it, studying it, meditating in it and listening to those who teach and preach it with authority and power. As God's Word gets into you, you digest it and it transforms your life. Jesus declared His Father to be the source of His life and He is the source of your life too. If you feed on other things more than you feed on God's Word, you are living a lower life than what God wants you to live. By not feeding on God's Word, you are feasting on death. Change your diet and eat His Word. It's sweet, delicious and life changing.

In Matthew 4:4 Jesus said, "Man shall not live by bread alone but by every word that proceeds from God's mouth." You can live by God's Word. God's Word gives you a better quality of life. Have a Bible feast. There is a smorgasbord of books and stories to feed on. Jesus' crucified body and His shed blood paved a clear path straight to God the Father. Get connected with Him today! Feed on His Word and live for Him.

Prayer: Heavenly Father, I thank You that you are my life. I live because of You. You are my desire. Your word is my spiritual food and I eat it because it is my daily bread. I ask you to come into my life. Lead, guide and direct me and show me where to go and how to live right. Father, I change my diet and I stop feeding on useless things. I commit to eat your word day and night. It is sweet and satisfying to me. I love your word.

11
CONNECT BY SAYING YES TO HIS INVITATION TO COME TO HIM

John 6:65 He said, "This is why I told you that **no one can come to Me unless it is granted to him by the Father.**"

John 14:6-7 Jesus told him, "I am the way, the truth & the life. **No one comes to the Father except through Me.** 7 "If you know Me, you will also know My Father. From now on you do know Him & have seen Him."

I love to receive invitations to events and parties because I love to be included where good things are happening. Every invitation that I ever received always requested me to RSVP, or respond very promptly, letting the one who invited me to know if I would or would not attend the event. If my schedule cooperated, I always answered yes to the invitation. God is also asking you to respond promptly to His invitation to come to Him through Jesus so you can connect with Him. Wherever the Father is, the fun is sure to be.

Anyone can come to God because He is always drawing people to Himself inviting them into His presence and granting them access to come before His throne of grace. God's invitation to come to Him has gone into the world and He accepts anyone who responds to this invitation by faith. You accept God's invitation by trusting in Jesus.

Jesus came from the Father and He leads you to His Father. Jesus is the perfect image of God. He revealed the Father to the world through His words, His actions and the love He showed mankind. To know Jesus is to know His heavenly Father.

You can know Jesus by faith, by believing in your heart that He is everything He said He is and by believing in the works He did. When you know Jesus, you can hang out with His Father. As you hang out with the Father, you can participate and enjoy in all that heaven has to offer. Your connection to God gives you full joy, a steadfast love that never fails and everlasting life.

Prayer: Father, I come to You in the name of Jesus. Thank You for drawing me to you. I boldly come into Your presence and am grateful that You have given me access to You. Father, I believe Your Word is the absolute truth and I trust You with all my heart. Please work in my life and lead me to the solid Rock that is higher than I. I choose to let Your will be my will and I will obey what You say. Help me to do the work You assigned to me and respond to Your invitation with joy.

☐

12
CONNECT THROUGH TEACHING AND SEEKING HIS GLORY

John 7:16-18 Jesus answered them, "My teaching isn't Mine but is from the One who sent Me. 17 **If anyone wants to do His will, he will understand whether the teaching is from God or if I am speaking on My own**. 18 The one who speaks for himself seeks his own glory. But He who seeks the glory of the One who sent Him is true, and there is no unrighteousness in Him.

John 8:50 I do not seek My own glory. There is One who seeks it, and He is the Judge.

To seek God's glory is to value, exalt and honor Him. You place His purposes and plans above your own. You look for ways to please God. You live for Him.

Everything Jesus did He did to please and obey His Father. Jesus did not seek His own glory, but He sought the glory of His Father. The works Jesus did, the healings people received, the miraculous provisions that occurred and the lives that were forever changed brought glory to God. Follow Jesus' example and seek God's glory, do what He wants and fulfill His desires and that will bring you close to the heavenly Father.

By teaching His Father's lessons Jesus glorified His Father. I am glad for the teachers that God put in my life who taught me about the Word of God, how to give God glory by applying the principles of heaven and truths about God's kingdom. I have learned so much about God and I am inspired to continue to go after God and glorify Him in all that I do. I really want my life to please the Lord and to connect with Him.

The teachings of Jesus are priceless, timeless truths that must be heard. Jesus was authorized & affirmed by God and when He taught, people connected with His Father. He was and is the greatest teacher of all time. Jesus captivated multitudes and explained truths about His kingdom through natural things like sheep, wells and farming. He taught the world how to get to God. His teaching glorified God and through His teachings you will understand God the Father.

Prayer: Heavenly Father I desire to honor you and enjoy your splendor. Give me insight to continue to learn about You. Please give me wisdom and help me to understand You and Your kingdom through Your Word. I delight myself in You. I love Your Word and it feeds my soul. Your Word is life and light. I honor Your Word and I seek to give You glory. Father Your Word is my treasure.

13
CONNECT BY KNOWING JESUS UP CLOSE AND PERSONAL

John 8:19 Then they asked Him, "Where is Your Father?" "You know neither Me nor My Father," Jesus answered. "**If you knew Me, you would also know My Father**."

How well can you know a person? You can choose to know a person very well or only a little. It all depends on how much time, effort and energy you are willing to invest. Relationships have many different levels. You may have close friends, acquaintances or not so close friends. You also may have relatives whom you see daily, occasionally or once in a great while. If you are married, you should have the closest relationship and know each other the best and God should be reflected by your marriage.

To know Jesus is to know His Father. The Son reflects the Father. Jesus didn't just look like His Father, He represented Him in the way He talked, the way He loved people, how He demonstrated His Faith and the miracles He did. Jesus was the express image of His Father and He represented His Father in every way. If you saw Jesus, you saw God. There was no better image of God on the earth than Jesus. Jesus and His Father were perfectly joined together as one.

Perhaps you would like to increase your intimacy with God? You can do that by increasing your intimacy with Jesus. You can read how He lived and what He did in the four gospels in the Bible. The more you know about Him, the more you will love Him.
Allow God to be involved in every part of your life by

getting to know Jesus better. Your life will be enriched by Him and you will be connected to your heavenly Father in a greater way. He is the most important person you need to be in a relationship with. Jesus invested His life into you because He considered you worthy and valuable. You can now invest your life in Him and receive an incredible return. He is waiting to reveal Himself to you and looks forward to spending time with you.

Prayer: Heavenly Father I want Jesus to be my friend. I give you my life and I ask You to give me Yours. I open my heart to know Jesus more. I purpose in my heart to seek the Lord. I acknowledge Him in all my ways, and I desire that He direct my paths. Be the Lord of my life and I surrender control to you. I love you Lord and I love you Father. In the name of Jesus.

14
CONNECT BY FAITH THAT PLEASES HIM

John 8:29 The **One who sent Me is with Me. He has not left Me alone, because I always do what pleases Him.**" 30 As Jesus spoke these things, many believed in Him.

Are you concerned about pleasing God? Do you intentionally strive to please Him on purpose? Has God provided you with something that will help you please Him, perhaps a useful tool to accomplish such a task? Yes, He has. Because if Jesus can please the Father, then you can too. The Lord provided you with more than a single tool, He has given you a toolbox that you can use to please Him. God has given you His Word, His Spirit, His faith and His Son to help you please Him. Faith is a necessary ingredient to connect with God and to please Him.

Faith pleases God by believing His Word is true, by recognizing God's character is trustworthy, by doing what God says and by carrying out His commands. Jesus gives you the faith you need to please God and He shows you how to use the faith that He gives to you.

One who operates in genuine faith will demonstrate these noticeable qualities in how they express their faith; love, joy, peace, longsuffering, kindness, goodness, faithfulness, gentleness and self-control.

Faith came to Jesus as His Father taught Him the Word. Jesus teaches you the same Word His Father taught Him through the Holy Spirit. Jesus believed His Father and acted on every word His Father spoke to Him, thereby always pleasing Him. As you hear God's Word, faith is produced in your heart and you can choose to believe what you heard from Him and please God just like Jesus did.

Prayer: Father, in Jesus' name I thank you that You have given me the spirit of faith whereby I believe and speak according to what is written in the Bible. Father, You strengthen my faith and help it grow. I commit to living by faith every day. I will walk by faith and not by sight. I thank You Lord that Your Word is my faith food and it directs my life.

15
CONNECT BY SPENDING TIME IN HIS PRESENCE

John 8:37 I know you are descendants of Abraham, but you are trying to kill Me because My word is not welcome among you. 38 **I speak what I have seen in the presence of the Father**; therefore, you do what you have heard from your father."

Imagine if you could speak with the King of kings anytime you wanted to? Wouldn't that be incredible? If you have accepted Jesus as your Savior and Lord, that dream has become a reality. You have an open invitation to come into His presence anytime and it is a great place to connect with your heavenly Father.

Everyone who believes in Jesus can come into God's presence confidently. This confidence comes from what Jesus accomplished in His life, death and resurrection. If you believe that Jesus Christ is God's Son, the Father welcomes you into His throne room, the most holy place. In His presence you can worship Him, talk with Him, receive instructions and correction and have fun. God is full of life. The more you spend time in God's presence the more enjoyable it will be for you.

You may be wondering how you can know you are connected to God? If you are connected to God you will spend time with Him, and you will have a story to tell and a desire to tell it to everyone you encounter. God will speak to you and share His heart, His truths and His plans with you. It is like being part of a close family. You spend time with family and share with them things about your life. If you are not connected to God, you will have nothing to share about Him, His kingdom or His nature.

God's presence is exciting and overflowing with life. It is so good to be in His presence that you won't be silent about it. Jesus has a direct line to the Father and He always had something to say that would change people and improve their circumstances. When you are connected to God, He will work through you and speak through you in order to help others.

You should spend quality time with God daily. Don't see it as a duty but a privilege. Spending time with God will keep you on the right path and cause you to be successful. Interacting with your heavenly Father is the most important priority of your daily life in order to stay connected. Enter God's presence and stay a while and see what happens.

Prayer: Heavenly Father, I humble myself and I come to You. You are my all in all. I need You and I receive the love You have for me. I want to share my heart with You as You share Yours with me. I look to You Lord, You are the Author and Finisher of my faith. I am listening to You, I believe in You and I trust in You.

16
CONNECT WITH YOUR HEAVENLY FATHER BY EMBRACING THE TRUTH

John 8:39-42 39 "Our father is Abraham!" they replied. "If you were Abraham's children," Jesus told them, "you would do what Abraham did. 40 But now you are trying to kill Me, a man who has told you the truth that I heard from God. Abraham did not do this! 41 You're doing what your father does." "We weren't born of sexual immorality," they said. "We have one Father — God." 42 Jesus said to them, "**If God were your Father, you would love Me, because I came from God** and I am here. For I didn't come on My own, but He sent Me.

John 8:43-45 Why don't you understand what I say? Because you cannot listen to My word. 44 You are of your father the Devil, and you want to carry out your father's desires. He was a murderer from the beginning and has not stood in the truth, because there is no truth in him. When he tells a lie, he speaks from his own nature, because he is a liar and the father of liars. 45 Yet because I tell the truth, you do not believe Me.

Which father influences you the most, the Father of truth or the father of lies? The one you listen to is the one who influences you. God is the Father of truth and Satan is the father of lies. Jesus was directly influenced by His Father's truth. He spoke truth and He is the Truth. When you love truth, you love Jesus and you are connected to His Father. Jesus is the Word of God made flesh and His truth is the Bible. You will find His Word to be trustworthy, powerful and transforming.

The other father, Satan, cannot come into God's presence for he was kicked out of heaven and he does not stand for the truth. The truth declared him to be the "father of liars." It is his nature to lie and he has zero truth in him. Along with being the father of liars he was also a murderer from the beginning. He possesses a hateful, rebellious murderous heart. The devil deceptively influences people through the world's system. What he says perverts, contradicts and disagrees with God's Word. You can tune his lies out and you can tune into God's truth simply by changing what you listen to. Let God's Word be your truth filter. If what you hear whether it's a voice, a preacher or anyone else, and it disagrees with God's Word, it's a lie so you can reject it.

Prayer: Father, I love Your Word. Jesus, You are my Savior and my source of truth. I believe in and receive Your truth and it makes me free. I tune my ears to Your Word and it filters out Satan's lies. You are my Father and I am committed to You. I love You with all my heart, soul and strength in Jesus' Name.

17

CONNECT BY HONORING HIM WITH YOUR TIME, TALENT & TREASURE

John 8:49-51 "I do not have a demon," Jesus answered. "On the contrary, **I honor My Father** & you dishonor Me. 50 **I do not seek My glory**; the One who seeks it also judges. 51 I assure you: If anyone keeps My word, he will never see death — ever!"

Jesus honors His Father by valuing Him, esteeming Him and holding Him in the highest regard. How do you honor God? How much do you value God by investing your time, talent and treasure into His work and kingdom?

Jesus gave His Father the best of Himself, His time, talent and treasure. Jesus honored His Father His entire life, in His birth, how He lived, what He gave, and He never quit till It was all finished. Love and joy motivated Jesus in giving His all to His Father

Honor exalts God for His rank, Almighty God. Honor values His character, He is perfect in all His ways. Honor respects His Word and puts it into practice. Knowing God as your Father is worth more than the most valuable precious stone or all the gold in the world. As you honor God you will reap His blessing.

I have found great joy in honoring the Lord. When I choose to value Him, He blesses me in numerous ways. It is my pleasure to honor my Father because He forgave me, He loves me, and He saved me from hell. I will stand in awe of Him all my life.

Jesus is the only One Who saved mankind from sin. He

honored God with His life, death and resurrection. He is worthy to be praised, worshiped and respected. God honors those who honor His Son and despises those who despise Him. The way to honor God is by giving Him your time, talent and treasure, freely and without question whenever He asks. There is great joy in honoring your Father in heaven.

Prayer: Heavenly Father, teach me how to be more honorable to you. Give me insight and understanding about what honor is and how to do it that pleases you. I am willing to honor you by putting you first in everything. I value God as the most precious person in my life by honoring Jesus and Holy Spirit. Thank you, Father for your help and strength in Jesus' Name.

18
CONNECT WITH YOUR HEAVENLY FATHER BY REJOICING IN HIM

John 8:54-56 "If I glorify Myself," Jesus answered, "My glory is nothing. My Father - you say about Him, 'He is our God' - He is the One who glorifies Me. 55 You've never known Him, but I know Him. If I were to say I don't know Him, I would be a liar like you. But I do know Him & I keep His word. 56 Your **father Abraham was overjoyed that he would see My day; he saw it & rejoiced**."

When you are connected to the Lord, an overwhelming joy fills your heart. The Lord is the source of joy and rejoicing. His joy is a source of strength for your life. When the Lord touches my heart I often respond with laughter. It is an unspeakable joy that flows out of the depth of my being. It has often resulted in what I call, "laughing spells". People who know me can testify of my laughing spells. They have occurred publicly and privately. One of the ways I know that I am connected to God is I have joy and I rejoice in Him often. You can overdose in joy without any harmful side effects.

Jesus was connected to His Father because He kept His Father's Word. Jesus trusted what His Father said about everything. It was a joy for Jesus to do what His Father commanded Him to do. Jesus was not sad, depressed or in despair about fulfilling His Father's plan. There was even joy before Him as He faced the cross. That joy was seeing the many people, all who called on Him to be saved, believe in Him and connect to His Father.

God enabled Abraham to see into the future and He saw God's Son, Jesus, giving His life as a sacrificial lamb. Abraham saw it and rejoiced. He was not disappointed, but he was overjoyed. He probably had more joy than was considered normal. Jesus brings joy, great joy and causes everyone who believes in Him to rejoice. It is very exciting and fulfilling to know the Lord and be connected to God your Father.

Prayer: Father, I come to you in Jesus' name. I see how valuable Your Word is and I purpose in my heart to keep Your Word. Your Word is my rock and fortress and it cannot fail. It brings joy to my heart and makes my path straight. I trust Your Word. Your Word gives me true freedom and is my light when things are dark. Continue to reveal Your Word to me in Jesus' name.

19

CONNECT BY GIVING YOUR LIFE TO HIS CAUSE

John 10:14-18 "I am the good shepherd. I know My own sheep, & they know Me, 15 as the Father knows Me, and I know the Father. I lay down My life for the sheep. 16 But I have other sheep that are not of this fold; I must bring them also, & they will listen to My voice. Then there will be one flock, one shepherd. 17 This is why the Father loves Me, because I am laying down My life so I may take it up again. 18 No one takes it from Me, but I lay it down on My own. **I have the right to lay it down, and I have the right to take it up again. I have received this command from My Father.**"

What cause would you give your life for? What do you live for? Do you desire to save the planet, or protect children, or protect animals, or change the world through politics or through entertainment or perhaps simply make a lot of money, etc.? Many people, all over the world, give themselves, their time, resources and life to causes that have no eternal value. Jesus gave Himself to a cause that had the highest eternal value.

Jesus truly is the Good Shepherd, something He learned from His Father. Just as a shepherd makes sure His flock is safe, well-fed and rested, God made the heavens and the earth and provided for mankind everything he needed, wanted and desired. He set up man for success. Jesus' cause was to save you and the world from sin. That cause cost Him His life but also gave Him a resurrection.

Our Father in heaven loves and appreciates when you give to His cause and blesses and rewards you. Jesus's Father gave Him the name above every name and exalted Him to the highest position for His sacrifice and commitment to follow through. He loves when people commit their lives to Him. Jesus followed His Father from heaven to earth, through the suffering and shame of the cross, to the grave and to the glorious resurrection. No challenged He faced could disrupt His connection with His Father. Since Jesus gave His life for you, consider giving your life to Him and follow through with what He has given to you to do.

Prayer: Heavenly Father, I lay down my rights and my life for you. You are my life and I am trusting you with all my heart. I love you with the love You gave me. I trust You and I lean not on my own understanding, but I acknowledge You in all my ways, so You may direct my path. You are my Good Shepherd. You are the Potter and I am Your clay, mold me and fashion me into what you want me to be.

20
CONNECT BY BEING ONE WITH HIM

John 10:27-29 "My sheep hear My voice, I know them & they follow Me. 28 I give them eternal life & they will never perish - ever! No one will snatch them out of My hand. 29 My Father, who has given them to Me, is greater than all. No one is able to snatch them out of the Father's hand. 30 **The Father & I are one.**"

I am a married man, married to a wonderful woman. There is a mystery that unfolds in a marriage, where two people can become one flesh. They share their thoughts, desires, hopes and dreams and they experience the highest degree of intimacy that people can share, becoming one flesh. After a while, a close couple can even finish each other's sentences. In becoming one, you develop a strong connection to each other.

You can become one with God like Jesus did. It begins with a desire to know God. A relationship with God is interactive and responsive. You need to seek Him, know Him, follow Him, communicate with Him and obey Him. God will ask you questions, correct you and challenge you and reveal things to you. You can also ask Him questions, share your heart with Him, your good moments and bad moments and He will listen to you. Be real and open with Him because you cannot fool Him anyway and He loves you.

Jesus declared that His Father is greater than all. Jesus gave His Father attention, respect, reverence and obedience. Jesus always gave His Father first place in His life which caused Him always to triumph at everything He did. Jesus has no failed attempts at pleasing God, and He has no losses on his record. You can be as successful as the Lord was by being one with Him. He gives you the grace, strength and leadership you need to follow His example.

Jesus willingly sacrificed His life to have a relationship with you and He guards that relationship very closely. Having a relationship with your Heavenly Father is the most precious and valuable relationship you can have. Protect your relationship with Him like He does with you. Make your relationship with God the number one priority in your life. The rewards and benefits are everlasting.

Prayer: Heavenly Father I come to You in Jesus' name and I desire to be one with You. I want to unite with Your plan, do Your will and learn about you. Father, I turn my heart to You, and I respect You, praise You and will obey You. I give You my all in Jesus' name.

21

CONNECT BY BEING THANKFUL THAT HE HEARS YOU

John 11:41-42 So they removed the stone. Then Jesus raised His eyes and said, "**Father, I thank You that You heard Me.** 42 **I know that You always hear** Me, but because of the crowd standing here I said this, so they may believe You sent Me."

Have you ever taken a moment to consider how good God is? God is good all the time. As I look back over my life, I can see how God worked things out, was kind to me, forgave me, loved me, protected me, delivered me and constantly was good to me. I am extremely grateful for God's goodness and faithfulness to me and I thank Him every day. God has always been a good listener to me as I shared my heart with Him.

Jesus stood at the tomb of His close friend Lazarus, who had been dead for four days, and He prayed this prayer, "Father, I thank you that You heard Me. I know that You always hear Me." He spoke this way for the benefit of the crowd that heard Him.

Faith is thankful that God hears its prayers. It is a good thing when you know God hears you. Jesus was grateful that His Father heard Him, and He appreciated the connection He had with His Father. How confident are you that God always hears you? The closer you are to God the easier it is to communicate with Him and to hear His voice and for Him to hear you when you pray. If you are not persuaded that God hears you, move closer to Him. Read His Word, praise Him for who He is and talk with Him and listen. He desires to talk with you.

God speaks the language of His Word and you can thank Him for helping you understand what He says. The Bible is God's love letter to you. God's Word is His will. Give God thanks that He enables you to speak God's Word back to Him so you can be assured that He hears you. God looks to perform His Word. When Jesus spoke to God, it was God's Word returning to Him because Jesus is the Word made flesh. Jesus loved talking with His Father, listening to Him and He was very thankful that His Father heard Him.

Prayer: Father, thank you for filling me with the knowledge of your will with all wisdom and understanding. Your will makes me confident in praying to You and I know You always perform Your will. I ask that the Spirit of God teach me and help me to understand the will of God. I am committed to doing Your will Father, in Jesus' name.

22
CONNECT BY FOLLOWING JESUS AND SERVING HIM

John 12:25-26 The one who loves his life will lose it; the one who hates his life in this world will keep it for eternal life. 26 If anyone serves Me, he must follow Me. Where I am, there My servant also will be. **If anyone serves Me, the Father will honor him**.

Who do you serve? You could serve many things such as God, yourself, the world, material things and even the devil. There is only one thing that will connect you to your heavenly Father and has an eternal reward and that is serving Jesus. Losing your life is laying down your dreams and desires and investing your life in fulfilling God's dreams and desires.

God honors those who choose to serve and follow His Son, Jesus. Following and serving Jesus requires love and commitment. One day, when Jesus was walking along the shore, He encountered two brothers who were fishermen, Peter and Andrew. He asked them to follow Him and He would make them fishers of men. These two brothers were intrigued and left all and began to follow and serve Jesus. They learned how to minister like Jesus and even worked miracles and performed wonders. They became mighty apostles who were instrumental in building the Lord's church.

I remember when I was younger and longing to serve the Lord. I would pray, "Father, wherever you want me to go, I will go; whatever you want me to do, I will do and whatever you want me to be, I will be." He showed me what to do and I did it and have been doing it for many years. For me, serving the Lord is very exciting!

To effectively serve Jesus, make Him your number one priority by putting Him at the top of your life and make yourself available to Him every day. You need to go where Jesus goes and do what He does. As you serve and follow the Lord, He will never disappoint you, fail you or let you down. He makes Himself known to you and works with you.

Prayer: Father, I thank you for Jesus. I dedicate and commit my life to follow and serve Him. Lord, I give you my all. I invest my life and put You first. You rescued me from sin, and I want to follow You and serve You all my days. I give to You all that I am. I love You Lord. Please continue to lead, guide and order my steps in Jesus' name.

23

CONNECT BY HAVING FAITH IN HIM AND IN HIS WORD

John 12:44-47 Jesus cried out, "**The one who believes in Me believes not in Me, but in Him who sent Me**. 45 The one who sees Me sees Him who sent Me. 46 I have come as a light into the world, so that everyone who believes in Me would not remain in darkness. 47 If anyone hears My words & doesn't keep them, I do not judge him; for I did not come to judge the world but to save the world. John 14:1 "Your heart must not be troubled. **Believe in God; believe also in Me**.

Your relationship with God begins when you believe that Jesus is God's Son, and you open your heart and invite Him to be your personal Lord. This brings you out of darkness and into the Lord's light and makes you a child of God.

Faith in God is what you believe about Him based in His Word, how you trust Him and how you follow His pattern of living and practice His divine principles. Believing in Jesus is having faith in God. Faith in God is how you receive from God.

Faith makes God's Word your "modus operandi" or MO. It is the reason you do what you do and the reason you live the way you live every day. Let God's Word govern your thoughts, words and actions and you will be joined with your heavenly Father.

God gave you His Word. The Word of God and the Son of God are synonymous. God's Word was given to you so that you could connect with Him. The Bible is all true, trustworthy and reliable and you can believe it, it's been tried and proven. History and science continue to affirm it. Have faith in both God's Word and Him to make your connection strong with Him.

Prayer: Father, in the name of Jesus, I proclaim my belief in You and in Your Word and accept it as the absolute truth. Your Word is my light to lead me out of darkness. I choose to honor Your Word and I will live by Your commands. Thank You for giving me Your Word. I will let Your Word be the standard of my life to follow and uphold all my days in Jesus' Name.

24
CONNECT BY LOVING JESUS & KEEPING HIS WORD

John 14:19; 23-24 "In a little while the world will see Me no longer, but you will see Me. Because I live, you will live too. 20 In that day you will know that I am in My Father, you are in Me and I am in you. 21 **The one who has My commands and keeps them is the one who loves Me. The one who loves Me will be loved by My Father.** I also will love him & will reveal Myself to him." 23 Jesus answered, "If anyone loves Me, he will keep My word. My Father will love him, & We will come to him & make Our home with him. 24 The one who doesn't love Me will not keep My words. The word that you hear is not Mine but is from the Father who sent Me.

Has anyone ever asked you to prove you love God? How can you prove you love the Lord? You can prove that you love God by keeping God's commands or by simply doing what He says. Jesus made it clear when He said, "The one who has My commands and keeps them is the one who loves Me. The one who loves Me will be loved by My Father." You are connected to your heavenly Father by keeping His Word.

Are you as close to God as you want to be, or would you like to be even closer? The Father loves those who love Him, and He makes His home in them. Imagine the power, the peace, the joy and love that comes to you when God your Father and God the Son reside in you. God's presence in you is awesome and it changes your life!

I am so glad that I connected to Jesus through obeying what He commanded me to do. I know that He loves me, and He knows that I love Him. I have benefited and have been enriched by God's abiding presence in my life. He has guided and led me to different places to work for Him and He has worked in me making me more like Jesus. He led me to Bible School where He trained me for the ministry He assigned to me. The Lord may not have led you to Bible School, but He has something just for you to do. I have done my best to follow the Lord's commands and I am thankful for being connected to My Father God.

God gives you a lifetime to build a relationship with Him. It doesn't matter if you entered a relationship with the Lord when you were young or older, you probably have discovered the richness of the Lord being at home in you.

Prayer: Heavenly Father, help me to love Jesus more and more. I am fully committed to keep Your Word in my heart and do it in my life. I thank you for giving to me this gift which produces eternal life. I receive Jesus into my heart and will follow Him all the days of my life. Lord I boldly declare that I love You.

25
CONNECT WITH GOD AS YOUR FATHER BY GLORIFYING JESUS

John 13:31 When he had gone out, Jesus said, "**Now the Son of Man is glorified and God is glorified in Him**. 32 If God is glorified in Him, God will also glorify Him in Himself and will glorify Him at once.

God gave us His only Son, the greatest gift to all the world and we should value Him for who He really is. There have been many who recognized Him, acknowledged Him and accepted Him into their hearts. All people who have done this have glorified Him or honored Him. To glorify Jesus is to worship, adore and exalt Him. There are also many who do not acknowledge Him, worship Him nor accepted Him into their hearts. These do not glorify the Lord. Which group do you belong to? You can connect with the heavenly Father by taking a moment by glorifying Jesus or honoring Him.

Jesus is the only way to get to the Father and touch His heart. How you speak of Jesus, relate to Jesus, worship Jesus and follow Him determines the strength of your connection you have with His Father. Jesus represents God's divinity and man's humanity and He is the only bridge that leads to God the Father. Jesus is called the Son of Man and the Son of God. God honors Jesus, Jesus honors God and all who honor Jesus are honored by His Father.

If you received Jesus as Lord, you willingly gave up control of your own life and submitted to Jesus' leadership. Because Jesus is your Lord, honor for Him, His Father and

His kingdom flows out of you freely. You cannot stop praising Him for His goodness, faithfulness, grace and love. You could thank God every day for a lifetime and He would always show you something else that would spark praise for Him in you.

When you know Jesus and believe His story, you will have an abundance of glory to give to Him. God is so good that you will be able to praise Him all your days and throughout eternity and you will never be tired of glorifying Him. Glorify the Lord and enhance your connection to your heavenly Father.

Prayer: Father, I come to you in Jesus' name. I recognize, honor and acknowledge Jesus as my Lord. Jesus, I need You in my life. I cannot get to where I need to be without You. Please lead, guide and direct me on the path of righteousness. Help me to represent Your kingdom well. I surrender to You and come to You and receive all that you have for me. Thank you for Your faithfulness in saving me. I commit to faithfully follow You and connect to my heavenly Father.

26
CONNECT BY ALLOWING HIS SPIRIT TO COUNSEL YOU

John 14:16-17 I will ask the Father & **He will give you another Counselor to be with you forever**. 17 He is the Spirit of truth.

Jesus asks His Father to give you another Counselor who will help you and will abide with you forever. God's Holy Spirit is assigned to be with believers to counsel them in the affairs of life. If you have received Jesus Christ as Lord you have been given the greatest teacher and personal life coach that dwells in you, God's Holy Spirit. What an amazing privilege! God is a Spirit and we connect to Him through His Spiritual network.

When the Spirit of truth comes, allow Him to work in you however He needs to. Do not restrict His work and do not reject His counsel. He cannot lie, He will explain the Bible to you, and He will even show you things to come. Listen to His advice for He will always point you in the truth.

God gives His Spirit to you as a child of God and His Spirit continually gives you good things from the Father. Jesus had His Father's Spirit on Him and in Him. The Holy Spirit led Jesus to do amazing things like perform miracles, outsmart the enemy, position Him in the right place at the right time and help Him teach, preach and heal wherever He went. Jesus gives to you and all His followers this same Spirit to do for you what He did for Jesus. How amazing is it that Jesus shares the same Holy Spirit with you?

You will have no better adviser than God's Counselor. He

inspired the authors of the Bible to write about Jesus. He will show you the Father's treasure and reveal to you the Father's truth. He is your source of power, understanding and joy. Learn to hear the Spirit's voice and receive His counsel to have a strong connection to God as your Father.

Prayer: Father, I am so grateful that You have given me Your Holy Spirit. I receive, appreciate and value the counsel that He gives me. I give Him my utmost attention. I allow the Holy Spirit to have His way in me. I will follow His leading, guidance and direction. Lord Jesus I thank you for this wonderful gift You have given to me.

27
CONNECT BY REJOICING IN JESUS RETURNING TO HIS FATHER

John 14:28-31 You have heard Me tell you, 'I am going away & I am coming to you.' If you loved Me, you would have rejoiced that I am going to the Father, because the Father is greater than I. 29 I have told you now before it happens so that when it does happen you may believe. 30 I will not talk with you much longer, because the ruler of the world is coming. He has no power over Me. 31 On the contrary, **I am going away so that the world may know that I love the Father. Just as the Father commanded Me, so I do.**
John 16:28 I came from the Father & have come into the world. Again, **I am leaving the world & going to the Father.**"

I love traveling, visiting different places, experiencing different cultures, customs and eating different types of food. It is exciting. But there is something even more exciting to me and that is returning home to see the ones I love who may have stayed behind. We rejoice as we embrace and share our experiences together. Reuniting with your family brings great delight and rejoicing.

Imagine if you saw how Jesus finished His course and ascended to His Father. Jesus' ascension showed how He loved His Father. He finished His assignment and it was time to return home. Jesus went home with joy and confidence knowing He had pleased His Father in all things. Jesus' return to His Father should strengthen your faith in Him and connection to Him. Jesus came, did His Father's will in dying, rising again and returning to heaven at the age of 33. That is so incredible, He did all that for you!

When Jesus finished His redemptive work of the crucifixion and resurrection, His disciples had the privilege of watching Him ascend back home into the clouds, (Acts 1:9). They rejoiced to see Jesus return home and they soon focused on carrying on His mission. Now that Jesus was gone, these followers of Christ had to maintain their strong connection to God. They did that through prayer, fellowship, studying, witnessing, learning and experiencing the wonderful blessing of God pouring out His Spirit on all flesh on the day of Pentecost. Jesus gave you hope that when you finish your God-ordained course you will have a place in heaven with the Father forever.

Prayer: Father, I thank you that You are greater than all. I trust & believe in Your greatness. I commit to do whatever you command me to do. Thank You Father for loving me and giving to me Jesus. Jesus, have your way in my life. I surrender and yield to Your will. After I have done Your will, I desire to return to you & be united to You forever. Father I love you & look to Jesus as My Lord and Savior, in Jesus' Name.

28
CONNECT BY BEING FRUITFUL IN KINGDOM BUSINESS

John 15:1-2; 15-17 "I am the true vine & My Father is the vineyard keeper. 2 Every branch in Me that does not produce fruit He removes & He prunes every branch that produces fruit so that it will produce more fruit. 15 I do not call you slaves anymore, because a slave doesn't know what his master is doing. I have called you friends, because I have made known to you everything I have heard from My Father. 16 You did not choose Me, but I chose you. **I appointed you that you should go out and produce fruit and that your fruit should remain**, so that whatever you ask the Father in My name, He will give you.

The fruit that Jesus is talking about here is everything you do in partnership with Christ. It is how the Lord lives His life through your life and how you yield to what is eternal.

God connects with fruitful people, people who are interested and invested in promoting His kingdom. Jesus appointed you to go out and produce results for Him and He fully expects you to be effective in working in His business. It is the Lord's will for you to produce lasting fruit.

When Jesus is your Lord, you live to please Him, obey Him and follow Him in everything. He works in you and through you to help you flourish. You cannot increase for God apart from God. God is always looking to maximize your ability to produce in His kingdom and will prune you and remove things that are unproductive, stifling or perhaps dead so that you can be fruitful.

One thing that Jesus does to help you increase your harvest is He makes known to you everything He has heard from His Father. He gives His friends insight into His Father's heart, plans and vision. This will help you to be valuable because you will always know what God wants to do and where He wants to move. Only those who are connected to Jesus have access to such important information. Take this information He gives to you about His Father and go into the world to produce fruit for His kingdom. Ask your Father for whatever you need in Jesus' name and He will give it to you. That is powerful.

Prayer: Father, in Jesus' Name, I humble myself before you and ask you to help me be fruitful for You in my life. I want to please You and produce good things for Your kingdom. Please help me and strengthen me so I can maintain a strong connection to You. I love You Lord.

29
CONNECT BY BEING A TRUE DISCIPLE

John 15:7-8 If you remain in Me & My words remain in you, ask whatever you want & it will be done for you. 8 **My Father is glorified by this: that you produce much fruit & prove to be My disciples**.

A disciple of Jesus is a follower of Christ who learns: the way of Christ, how to operate in His kingdom, the doctrines of the Scriptures and the holy lifestyle that He promoted when He walked the earth. The gospels provide you with valuable information about Jesus' life, His work and how He lived. You must study God's Word, read it every day and meditate on what it says. The Holy Spirit will help you understand it and apply it. If you are committed to learning about the Lord Jesus you will experience a wonderful connection to your heavenly Father.

According to the Lord, there are two ingredients that are necessary for discipleship. First, you must remain in the Lord. Many people start a relationship with the Lord, but things enter their heart like loss of focus, trouble, persecution, worldly cares and covetousness. These can cause a person to stop following Jesus and follow something else. Commit your life to Jesus and remain committed to Him no matter what.

Secondly, the Lord's words must remain in you. You study God's Word to know it, apply it to your life and do it. God's Word governs your thoughts, words and actions and it becomes the reason you live the way you live. Others can look at you and see and hear God's Word flow out of you. These two ingredients are important for you being a good disciple and connecting with your heavenly Father.

A true disciple of the Lord has a close relationship with God, His Spirit and His Word. You don't have to tell everyone that you are a disciple of Jesus, you simply need to show them by how you live, how you speak and how you love. By putting action to God's Word, you will demonstrate to the world Whose you are and who you are. A disciple is simply a doer of what God said.

Prayer: Heavenly Father, I come before You and I love your Word. Your Word is life to me. I desire to read, hear, study and learn Your Word. Your Word makes my prayer powerful and effective. Continue to work in me and help me to be a great producer for Your kingdom. It is my desire to glorify You, Father, in Jesus' Name.

30
CONNECT BY REMAINING IN HIS LOVE

John 15:9-10 **"As the Father has loved Me, I have also loved you. Remain in My love.** 10 If you keep My commands you will remain in My love, just as I have kept My Father's commands & remain in His love.

Have you ever thought about how God loves you? What would cause a Father to give His only Son as a sacrificial lamb, to watch Him endure what Jesus had to endure, in order to save a people who disobeyed God and turned against Him? It must be true love. Yes, the Father loves you so much that He would do this for you to restore a close relationship with you! Jesus loves you the same way His Father loves Him, and He shares that love with you.

Jesus encourages you to remain in His love. God's love is so good, wonderful, gracious, kind and unfailing it's hard to fathom why anyone would want to leave it. How do you remain in God's love? You stick with Jesus. You stay connected to Him by following Him, praising Him, serving Him and doing His will.

When I think of a person who has remained in God's love and followed Him his whole life, I think of Billy Graham. He did what God wanted him to do and he stuck with it. He impacted several generations and from the moment he made Jesus His Lord until he left this earth, he remained in God's love.

The key to remaining in the Lord's love is keeping His commands. God's book, the Bible, reveals who He is, what His kingdom is about and His purposes and plans for mankind. The Bible is the will of God, God's gift to you and it is Jesus from cover to cover. You remain in God's love by keeping His Word your whole life and you will be connected to your heavenly Father forever.

Prayer: Heavenly Father, I thank You for loving me. You showed Your love for me by giving Jesus to me. I choose to love You and connect to Your love. I will remain in Your love. I love Your Word and it is real to me. Thank You for speaking to me through Your Word. It is my life source. Thank you, Lord, for drawing me close to You in Jesus' Name.

31
CONNECT BY TESTIFYING ABOUT HIM

John 15:26-27 When the Advocate comes, whom I will send to you from the Father—the Spirit of truth who goes out from the Father—He will testify about Me. 27 **And you also must testify, because you have been with Me from the beginning**.

The Lord encourages you to testify about Him. To testify about the Lord, you must tell what you know, what you saw, what you heard and what you experience about Him. Your testimony is evidence of how good God is. Those who hear your testimony about Jesus could be influenced to become a follower of Jesus too. Your testimony could be the difference between life or death for someone who hears it. The more time you spend with Jesus the more good things you will experience that will enhance your testimony.

God is good, He provided us with a way of salvation, and He does good things for those who love Him. The works that the Lord does are good and worthy to be shared. I could say confidently that the Lord saved me from sin. I remember vividly when I accepted Jesus as my Lord. I felt His mercy and His love as they flooded my heart. I experienced God's presence rush into me like a strong wind blowing. I have testified of that truth hundreds of times over the past thirty-seven years. I have never tired of sharing that story with others. Hopefully, that testimony inspired others to invite the Lord into their hearts.

Testifying about what Jesus has done for you is like an advertising billboard. It promotes God's goodness and shows others to how good your heavenly Father was to you and how good He can be to all who see and hear the message. There is an exhilarating joy that comes when you share with others what God has done for you. It is as if God is smiling over you as you share. Testify about the Lord and connect with your heavenly Father.

Prayer: Heavenly Father, I come to you in the name of Jesus and I thank you that I am rooted and grounded in your love. Lord, I allow You to work in me however You desire. You are the Potter and I am the clay so have Your way in me. I will proclaim the goodness of God all my days.

32
CONNECT BY RECEIVING WHAT HIS SPIRIT DISCLOSES

John 16:12-15 I still have much to tell you, but you cannot yet bear to hear it. 13 However, when the Spirit of truth comes, He will guide you into all truth. For He will not speak on His own, but He will speak what He hears, and He will declare to you what is to come. 14 **He will glorify Me by taking from what is Mine and disclosing it to you**. 15 **Everything that belongs to the Father is Mine**. That is why I said that **the Spirit will take from what is Mine and disclose it to you**.

Have you ever wondered where Father God keeps His treasure? He keeps His treasure in His Son who possesses all that His Father owns. Jesus has the full amount of His Father's fullness, wisdom, knowledge, power, gifts and glory. The Son of God is equal with His Father and they have a most intimate union with each other. It is the Holy Spirit Who discloses to you what belongs to you in Jesus so you can receive it and share in it with the Lord. Open your heart and receive all that He tells you that you can have. He will show you how His grace works, He will teach you truth about your covenant and He will help you to defeat every enemy and so much more.

Jesus wanted to teach His disciples more about His Father's treasures, but they were not able to receive any more at that time. But Jesus knew they would be able to receive from His Spirit when He came, and He would disclose to them what they needed to know. God's Holy Spirit shares with you and declares to you the things that God has stored up for you in His treasure chest, Jesus. The Holy Spirit helps you to receive what belongs to you in Christ. He will reveal

God's secrets and help you understand His truth so you can walk in it.

God the Father connects with you through His Son by His Holy Spirit. God's Spirit is your personal tour Guide who directs you to receive from the Father's treasures in Jesus.

Only through the work of the Holy Spirit will you be able to understand and operate in the thousands of promises that God has made to you that are stored in His Word. You could think of the Holy Spirit as your transfer agent who keeps records of what God owns and who He has distributed His treasures to. He will solve any ownership problems. Everything God's Spirit declares to you is yours so take possession of it.

Prayer: Father, I come to You in the Name of Jesus. Please open my eyes that I may realize how great a treasure Jesus is. Thank You for giving Jesus to me. I receive Him and I believe Him. I allow Your Holy Spirit to show me what is mine. I can do nothing without You living and working in my life. Help me to share this treasure with others and I choose to follow Jesus all my days. Thank You Lord.

33
CONNECT BY BECOMING ONE WITH HIM

John 16:20-23 I pray not only for these, but also for those who believe in Me through their message. 21 **May they all be one, as You, Father, are in Me & I am in You. May they also be one in Us, so the world may believe You sent Me.** 22 I have given them the glory You have given Me. May they be one as We are one. 23 I am in them & You are in Me. May they be made completely one, so the world may know You have sent Me & have loved them as You have loved Me.

God desires you to be one with Him just like a husband and wife should become one when they are married. To be one with God is to draw close to Him, be intimate and open with Him. You share everything as you talk to Him like your thoughts, feelings, aspirations, failures, faults and victories. Jesus prayed for people like you who follow Him, to be one like He and the Father are one. We can follow His example.

God wants to be so closely connected to you that when people look at you, they see Him. It takes a strong trust to be that close to your Father. Jesus shares His glory with those who trust in Him. When you are one with the Lord you are one with the Father, and people will know that God sent you and they will experience God's love that resides in you and flows out of you. Jesus is the outlet where you plug into His Father and share in His love and power.

Jesus wants to exchange your junk for His goods. He wants you to be in Him and He wants to be in you. He will take your sins and give you forgiveness. He will take your darkness and give you light. He will take your hopelessness and give you divine hope. He will take your sorrow and give you His joy. He will take your weakness and give you His strength. Love the Lord, receive what He has for you and be one with Him.

Prayer: Father I thank you in the Name of Jesus for sharing Your Son and Your heart with me. I want to be one with You. I desire to draw closer and closer to You every day. I thank You that my life is woven with Yours and the life I now live, I live by faith in the Son of God. Thank you for not forsaking me but choosing me as Yours. I receive what Your Holy Spirit shows me and tells me. My ears are open to His voice and I am listening intently.

34
CONNECT BY PRAYING TO HIM IN JESUS' NAME

John 16:23-24 In that day you will not ask Me anything. "**I assure you: Anything you ask the Father in My Name, He will give you.** 24 Until now you have asked for nothing in My name. Ask and you will receive, so that your joy may be complete

When you accept Jesus as Lord, you are a joint heir with Him in everything. Whatever He has and received also belongs to you. Since you are a joint heir with Him, you have the right to ask Him anything. When you are aligned with Jesus, anything the Father has is available to you. Ask Him in the name of Jesus because that name is the Master key to everything that God has. Connect to your Father by regularly communicating with Him in prayer.

Father God is the greatest giver of all time. He has great joy in giving to His children. Whenever He gives, He gives lavishly, generously and abundantly. He wants you to have what you need, what you want and what you desire. He is not holding things back from you but shares every good thing with you when you ask Him in Jesus' name.

One of the benefits of receiving answers to your prayers is you have complete joy. Do you have complete joy? That is a joy that is full, rich, satisfying and needs nothing else. A complete joy is an overflowing joy. It surges out of you like a rushing river. You cannot contain it.

As a follower of Christ, you must become a good receiver. Since God is the greatest giver, He looks for people who can receive from Him. When you ask the Father for things that are within His will, He will give them to you in order to bless you. He is good to you because He loves you and He wants you to be joyful.

Prayer: Father, I thank You that I can pray, call upon You and communicate with You in the Name of Jesus. I am so grateful for Jesus and all that You do for me. I will follow You with all my heart, soul and strength. Father, You are good, and I praise You. I thank you that You are willing to give to me what I need, want and desire. I receive from you in Jesus' Name.

35
CONNECT BY BEING FAITHFUL TO THE END

John 17:1-5 Jesus spoke these things, looked up to heaven, & said: Father, the hour has come. Glorify Your Son so that the Son may glorify You, 2 for You gave Him authority over all flesh so He may give eternal life to all You have given Him. 3 This is eternal life that they may know You, the only true God, and the One You have sent — Jesus Christ. 4 **I have glorified You on the earth by completing the work You gave Me to do.** 5 Now, Father, glorify Me in Your presence with that glory I had with You before the world existed.

Are you prepared to go the distance and finish strong? It doesn't matter how you start but it does matter how you finish. Jesus carried out His Father's purpose fully and completely. Although He was tempted to quit, give up and turn away, He never did. He ended His earthly life on the cross and began a new life at His resurrection.

If you are determined to finish strong then you must avoid temptations and distractions that will pop up along the way. The Lord gives you a way out of every temptation and if you keep your eyes on Jesus being focused on His will, you will avoid distractions and win. You may have heard the phrase, "When the going gets tough, the tough get going." No matter how hard it seems or how tough it gets, you can be faithful to the end.

There is a joy that accompanies a strong finish. I remember years ago I ran a four-mile race. I completed it in about forty minutes. It was hard and there were times when I wanted to quit but oh, the joy I felt when I finished the race. I didn't place in the top ten, but I finished. I accomplished my goal and I was thrilled.

Father God celebrates those who complete His work. God completed His work of creation in six days then rested on the seventh day, a day to reflect on what was done. He celebrates strong finishers as they look back to see what they did. You can follow Jesus' example by being faithful to God till the end and connect to Your Father God. You can do what Jesus did and finish strong.

Prayer: Heavenly Father, I thank you that you have called me to Yourself and given me a divine assignment for my life. Thank you for strengthening me to carry out your will completely. I thank You that You lead, guide and direct me in the way that I should go. I am committed to doing Your will and glorifying You in all that I do. Work in me and work through my life. Help me to shine my light to the world in Jesus' Name.

36
CONNECT BY DRINKING THE CUP THAT HE GAVE YOU

John 18:11 Jesus said to Peter, "Sheathe your sword! **Am I not to drink the cup the Father has given Me?**"

What does it mean to drink the cup that the Father has prepared? It means to do all that God wants you to do. God's exclusive plan for Jesus was for Him to suffer on your behalf. Jesus fully embraced the fullness of God's plan for Him. It was not God's will for Jesus to resist being captured by physical force, to resist his painful beatings or to resist the cross. It was His time to yield to the suffering He was about to endure. Jesus willingly yielded to His Father's will and drank the cup He was given fully. Everyone's cup from the Father is specific, different from others and unique.

God has a will, a plan, a purpose and a cup for you. If you believe in Him, He will show you your own cup. When you know what God's will is for you, you can choose to to carry it out no matter what you face along the way. Jesus credited His Father for giving Him this cup to drink from. Since this cup came from His Father, Jesus knew that He had the strength to endure it and be victorious over it no matter what. Jesus graciously agreed and accepted this as God's will. He wholly yielded to it and faced it courageously. Your Father also provides you with the strength to endure your cup which has nothing to do with sickness, evil or anything related to the devil.

Jesus was fully committed to His Father's will, even if He suffered. Drinking the Father's cup is humbly submitting to His will. That level of commitment, to do whatever God says and directs, produces a strong bond with the Father and will help you to face any obstacle and win over every challenge.

If you knew God gave you a cup that was hard to drink or endure would you still embrace it and do it? The tenderness with which the Father gave His Son this cup, removed the bitterness of the suffering He endured. Jesus delighted in pleasing His Father, so He embraced this cup and suffered, died, was buried but rose again on the third day.

Prayer: Heavenly Father, give me the strength and courage to accept, embrace and carry out Your will no matter what. Father, I yield to Your goodness. I know that Your plans for me are always good. Lord, I thank you for giving me sight to see beyond what is seen. I rely on Your strength and it is through Your strength that I am made strong. Father, I know that You will deliver me from every evil I may face in Jesus' Name.

37
CONNECT BY ASCENDING TO HIM IN PRAYER

John 20:17 "Do not cling to Me," Jesus said, "for I have not yet ascended to the Father. But go and tell My brothers, **'I am ascending to My Father and your Father, to My God and your God.'**"

Jesus is the great High Priest who passed through the heavens and presented Himself clean, whole and pure before His Father. He had to ascend to His Father, sprinkle His blood on God's mercy seat in the Most Holy Place so that the Father could put His stamp of approval on the finished work of Christ.

Jesus ascended to the Father as humanity's representative to be declared victorious over sin and death. His victory became your victory and of all who believe in and trust Him as Lord. Because He ascended to His Father, we can now come before the throne of grace with boldness to receive mercy and find grace to help us when we need it, (Hebrews 4:14-16). Jesus' ascension seals our connection with God as Father.

Jesus entered the Most Holy Place of heaven with His own blood and applied it on the throne of God to secure eternal redemption for us, (Hebrews 9:11-14). He appeared in God's presence for us, so we can appear in God's presence through prayer.

Jesus' ascension also solidified for us the ability to cleanse our consciences from dead works so that we may serve the Living God and strengthen our connection to Him.

When you pray to God in faith, your prayer is like incense that ascends to heaven. It reaches God's throne, touches His heart and causes Him to answer you. Jesus' death, resurrection and ascension gave you a direct line to God with no interruptions or interference. You can touch your Father's heart in prayer.

Prayer: Heavenly Father, I thank You that Jesus represented me and appeared before Your throne on my behalf. I draw close to You Father and I thank you that Your Holy Spirit helps me to pray effectively and to maintain my focus on You in the Name of Jesus.

ABOUT THE AUTHOR

Douglas Pyszka

Douglas Pyszka an ordained minister and is passionate about helping people from all walks of life to find their inheritance in the Word of God. He is an author and international speaker. He is also Lead Pastor at Victory Christian Fellowship, Palmyra PA. He is a graduate of Rhema Bible Training College and Lee University. He is married to Fiona and has two sons, Gabriel and Josiah. He and his family currently reside in Central Pennsylvania.

Other Books Include:
- Depth: Doing Excellent Principles of Truth With Honor
- An Everyday Hero: How to Develop The Hero Within
- The Outdoorsman: A Spiritual Survival Guide
- Exceed Limits and Break Barriers: UNDERSTANDING THE POWER OF WORDS

All books are available on Amazon.